Winds

of

Resilience

In every setback, there lies a whisper of a new beginning...

By

Vikash K Agarwal

Disclaimer

This novella is a fictional work. Names, characters, places, and incidents are the author's imagination. Any resemblance to actual persons, living or dead, or real events is purely coincidental. The work was also developed with the assistance of AI tools, which were used to support brainstorming and editing. All creative direction, narrative decisions, and final content are the author's sole responsibility.

Dedication

To the countless souls, both living and departed, who have inspired me in ways words can never fully capture.

To my wife, Shweta, for giving me the gentle push I needed to begin this journey.

And to my Mummy and Papa for the deep roots of wisdom, love, and resilience they planted in me.

Contents

Contents

Synopsis

"When dreams crumble and love fades, where do you find the strength to rise again?"

Winds of Resilience follows the journey of **Narayan**, a young man navigating life's unpredictable storms - from the tender promises of first love to the devastating blows of heartbreak and the relentless pursuit of ambition.

When his world falls apart, it is his father's steadfast wisdom and unwavering belief that become his guiding light. With every setback, **Narayan** discovers that resilience is not merely about enduring adversity but about embracing hope, rising after each fall, and finding new beginnings in the darkest moments.

Set against a vivid backdrop of cultural expectations and personal growth, **Winds of Resilience** is a profound tale of love, loss, and the quiet courage to rebuild. This novella will resonate deeply with anyone who has faced life's trials and found the strength to rise once more.

A tribute to the unyielding human spirit, this story reminds us that no matter how many times we fall, it is the courage to rise again that defines who we are.

* * * *

Preface

Life is a delicate tapestry woven with threads of joy, struggle, and moments that test the very essence of who we are. **Winds of Resilience** delves into this shared human experience - the quiet strength forged in adversity, the courage to love despite the pain, and the wisdom discovered in the depths of loss.

Through **Narayan's** journey, you will walk the dusty paths of childhood dreams, scale the steep ascents of ambition, and traverse the valleys of heartbreak. This story is a heartfelt tribute to the belief that resilience is not simply enduring life's storms but learning to embrace the present moment and grow through its trials.

Narayan's path, much like our own, is not a straight one. It twists, shatters, and rebuilds, reflecting the complexities of life itself. As you turn each page, may you see glimpses of your own struggles and victories, drawing strength from the indomitable spirit that propels us forward.

Let this novel be a gentle reminder: In every setback lies a seed of growth, and within every ending, the whisper of a new beginning. Embrace the winds of change - they carry you towards the horizon of your true self.

May you rise, time and time again, no matter how often you fall.

* * * * *

Chapter 1

When the Heart Shatters

The evening breeze filtered through the half-open window, carrying the scent of jasmine from the garden below. Narayan sat on the edge of his bed, his fingers gripping the phone so tightly that his knuckles turned white.

"Narayan, we have to end this." Angelina's voice trembled, but her words were firm.

His heart dropped. For a moment, he couldn't breathe. The world outside blurred into a swirl of muted colours. He swallowed hard and forced himself to speak.

"Angelina, please. Don't say that. You know I love you. We can work this out,"

A long pause crackled on the line.

"Narayan, love isn't enough. Our families... they'll never accept this. I can't fight them forever."

Her words cut through him, swift and unforgiving, like a sudden monsoon gust through a cracked window. How had they come to this moment? They'd dreamed of a future together, whispered plans under the shade of old banyan trees, and shared laughter that seemed to echo into eternity. Now, those dreams were crumbling before his eyes.

"Just give it more time," he pleaded, his voice breaking. "I know things will get better. We've come so far... please don't give up on us."

"I'm sorry," she said, her voice now a whisper. "I have to think about my family, my future. It's over, Narayan."

The line went dead with a cold, final click.

Narayan's hand fell to his lap, the phone slipping from his grasp. The silence in the room was deafening. He felt a hollow ache in his chest, a void where his heart used to be. Tears welled in his eyes, and he let them fall, unashamed.

He thought back to their first meeting, to her smile that felt like sunlight breaking through clouds. She'd seen something in him, something no one else had.

But now, that light was gone.

The hours blurred into the night, each second heavier than the last. His thoughts spiralled through memories of Angelina: the laughter, the whispered promises, the warmth of her touch. He clenched the pen, his body trembling like a paper boat adrift on a swollen river -helpless and fragile.

Words felt like the only way to make sense of the ache. He picked up a pen and let his heart bleed onto the page.

Narayan's tears fell freely, his heart splintered by the weight of her words. Yet, somewhere in the depths of his pain, a seed of resilience lay dormant, waiting for the right moment to push through the cracks. The embers of hope still glowed faintly, waiting to be reignited.

* * * * *

Chapter 2

Ink of Despair, Words of Hope

Night settled like a heavy blanket over Narayan's heart, each moment of silence amplifying his pain. Unable to hold back his anguish, he reached for a pen. Perhaps, in ink, he could find the words to make sense of his despair.

A Poem of Love and Hope

"I live every moment; I die every second.
Angelina, in your love, I count my every breath.
Whenever I am there with my feelings,
You always come into my thoughts.
With sweet experiences and moments of lovely dreams,
You go back after giving a peck.
You are there in the morning mist, you are there in the rustling neem leaves,
You are there in the stars that watch over my village; you are there in every prayer I give.
Every moment I feel just one name – Angelina,
And every sound says just this – Angelina, you are only mine.
I will wait for you,
For I believe in myself and I have faith in God.
This life or any life,
I will be only yours."

– Love you, my love

Night pressed on Narayan's chest like a stone, the pale moonlight barely piercing the darkness. He hadn't moved from his bed since the phone call ended. The silence was oppressive, broken only by the faint ticking of the wall clock.

But verses couldn't carry the full weight of his heartache. He needed someone to hear him, to guide him out of the darkness.

His fingers trembled as he reached for his pen and a blank sheet of paper. His heart was too full; his thoughts tangled like a web of thorns. He needed to unload this unbearable weight, to pour his emotions onto the page. And there was only one person he trusted to understand his pain - his father.

Letter to Papa

Dearest Papa,

Tonight, I feel shattered. The life I imagined, the love I cherished, has slipped away. Angelina ended our relationship. I feel like I'm standing on the edge of a cliff, like that day when I climbed the banyan tree and slipped. You caught me then, Papa. But now, I feel like there's no one to catch me.

She told me I'm too emotional and that I won't be strong enough to support her when things get tough. Papa, does feeling everything so deeply make me weak? Is there no place for emotions in survival? I loved her with every part of me, but it still wasn't enough.

I can't eat, I can't sleep. My thoughts are a fog, my heart a jagged, broken thing. How do I move forward, Papa? How do I keep going when everything that gave my life meaning has been torn away?

I'm scared to dream again, Papa. My dreams have turned into nightmares.

Your son,
Narayan

He folded the letter, tears smudging the ink, and slipped it into an envelope. His heart felt marginally lighter, though the ache throbbed with each beat.

Lying back down, he stared at the ceiling. Memories of Angelina engulfed him - the sparkle in her eyes when she laughed, the warmth of her hand in his. Each memory was a dagger, but he clung to them, terrified that letting go would mean losing her forever.

Letter from Papa

On the third day, a letter arrived. His father's familiar handwriting was like a steady hand on his shoulder.

Dearest Narayan,

I feel your pain, my son. The emptiness, the endless questions - I know them well. Love can bring the greatest joy but also the deepest wounds. Yet, it is in this very pain that you will discover your strength.

Feeling deeply does not make you weak; it makes you profoundly human. Those who dare to feel deeply also experience life fully. Your emotions are not a burden - they are a gift. They will fuel your resilience and anchor you when storms rage around you.

You ask how to move forward. The answer is simple, though not easy: one step at a time. Each breath, each sunrise, and each small effort will guide you toward healing. Life does not end with one loss, Narayan. It transforms, it adapts, and so will you.

Don't fear dreaming again. Dreams are seeds waiting to bloom. Plant them, nurture them, and trust that they will grow in time.

I believe in you, my son. You are stronger than you realise. This pain will shape you, but it will not define you. Rise from it like a phoenix from the ashes.

I am with you, always.

Your loving,
Papa

Narayan clutched the letter to his chest. His father's words were a balm on his wounded heart. For the first time in days, he felt a flicker of hope. The world hadn't ended; it had only changed. Maybe he could, too.

He let out a shaky breath and read the letter again, each word seeping into the cracks of his broken spirit. His father's belief in him felt like a lifeline, pulling him back from the edge. *"Feeling deeply does not make you weak."* The phrase echoed in his mind, softening the shame he'd felt for his emotions.

He closed his eyes and imagined his father's steady hand on his shoulder, the way it had felt when he was a boy, lost or frightened. That touch, that unwavering presence, had always guided him home. Maybe now, even without being there in person, his father's words could guide him back to himself.

A small, cautious warmth began to spread through his chest. It wasn't the blinding light of joy but a fragile ember of determination. He wasn't healed yet, but he wasn't drowning anymore.

He wiped his tears, a new resolve taking shape. His pain hadn't disappeared, but his father's words had shown him that pain could be a path, not just a wall. The journey ahead would be long and uncertain, but his father's belief in him was the light he needed to take that first step.

Perhaps, he needed to remember where he came from to find his way forward. As he clutched his father's letter, Narayan realised he needed to remember who he was before the heartbreak - a boy shaped by simpler times and quiet resilience.

Perhaps the answers lay in the roots he'd tried so hard to honour.

* * * * *

Chapter 3

Roots of Resilience

Part 1: Childhood Lessons

Narayan's father's steady words echoed in his mind, drawing him back to **Sukhpura**, where resilience was as much a part of life as the soil beneath his feet. The comforting wisdom, infused with love, seeped into his heart, soothing his ache - if only slightly. As he reread the final line, *"Rise from it, like a phoenix from the ashes,"*, a flood of childhood memories returned. They were recollections of simpler times when struggles were met with wide-eyed wonder and the steadfast support of his family.

A quiet strength stirred within him. His father's words took root, planting a seed of resilience. Narayan closed his eyes and let the memories of home wash over him. He saw Sukhpura - its dusty lanes, the steady shade of the neem tree, and the gentle lessons that had shaped his character. Perhaps the answers he was searching for lay buried in his roots.

Sukhpura was a village where bullock carts creaked along dusty paths and the aroma of freshly made chapatis blended with the earthy scent of cow dung cakes drying in the sun. Here, Narayan first encountered the quiet strength that now seemed so distant. Life in Sukhpura moved gently, wrapped in routine's comforting simplicity and close-knit families' warmth. For young Narayan, the village was his entire world, and each corner held a lesson waiting to be learned.

First Day of Education

On his first day of school, Narayan woke with excitement buzzing through his veins. His mother had laid out a neatly washed uniform - a half-sleeved shirt, blue shorts, and sandals worn from too many monsoons. The clothes smelled of fresh soap, a scent that comforted him. His father stood by the doorway, a proud smile stretching beneath his neatly combed hair.

"Ready to learn, beta?" his father asked, his voice rich with hope.

Narayan nodded eagerly. He didn't know what awaited him beyond the dirt path that led to the *pathshala* on the village outskirts, but the thrill of discovering something new was electric. Every letter traced, every number repeated, planted a seed of resilience – lessons that would stay with him long after the school bell faded.

The Neem-Shadowed Pathshala

The school was a simple building, its walls whitewashed and cracked in places, with a large neem tree providing much-needed shade. Inside, children sat on the floor, their voices a soft hum of curiosity and nervousness. The teacher, whom everyone called *Masterniji*, was a stern woman with a heart hidden beneath her rigid exterior. A long bamboo stick rested against the wall - both a tool for discipline and a reminder of the need for diligence.

Narayan took his place on a worn mat, his slate and chalk in hand. He watched *Masterniji* closely, repeating letters and numbers after her. The rhythm of learning took hold of his young mind. His fingers smudged with white dust; he practised until the characters looked just right. He wondered if he would ever catch up to the older boys.

At recess, he sat under the neem tree, eating the *roti* and jaggery his mother had packed. He listened as other children chattered, some forming groups, others playing marbles in the dirt. Narayan was shy, preferring the quiet companionship of his own thoughts, but he observed everything, storing away impressions like treasures in a chest.

In the rigid rules of the *pathshala*, Narayan unknowingly built the discipline and resilience that would become his armour in adulthood.

A Father's Determination

In the evenings, his father would sit with him, asking about his lessons.

"Did you learn something new today?" he'd ask, his eyes sharp with expectation.

Narayan would nod and show his slate, the numbers and letters carefully written. His father would smile, a quiet satisfaction settling in his eyes.

"Narayan, education is your key. Knowledge - once yours - can't be stolen."

His father's words sank deep into Narayan's heart. He knew his father's journey hadn't been easy - a man who had once lost everything in a fire and clawed his way back, building a small business from the ashes. Resilience was his father's gift, and Narayan accepted it without knowing its full weight.

From his school days to now, his father's unwavering belief in him was the one constant that had never faltered.

Footsteps of Tenacity

One monsoon day, Narayan tripped on his way to school, his slate shattering on the muddy road. Tears welled in his eyes as he looked at the broken pieces. He thought of the hours spent practising his writing, now lost in the rain-soaked mud.

He turned back, dreading his father's reaction.

His father listened quietly as Narayan, between sobs, explained what had happened. Instead of scolding him, his father gently placed a hand on his shoulder.

"It's just a slate, beta. What matters is what you've learned. The slate can be replaced, but your knowledge is yours forever."

Narayan wiped his tears, a small flame of determination flickering inside him. The next day, he returned to school with a new slate and a stronger resolve.

Under the Banyan Tree of Hopes

As the months passed, Narayan began to find his voice. He made a few friends, boys who shared his love for stories and dreams of a future beyond the village. They spent afternoons imagining lives as great businessmen, engineers, and adventurers.

But even in their games, Narayan's aspirations were different. While his friends dreamed of riches and fame, Narayan dreamed of understanding the world - not just how things worked, but why.

Under the neem tree, he often sat with his thoughts, the breeze rustling the leaves above him. He felt a quiet certainty that his path would be different, that he was meant to follow his heart, even if he didn't yet know where it would lead.

Back then, his dreams were unclouded by fear or doubt – simple visions of a future shaped by curiosity and hope.

A Foundation of Values

His school days passed in a blur of lessons, laughter, and small challenges that seemed monumental at the time. Each experience, each scrape, and each word of encouragement from his parents became a thread in the fabric of his character.

His father's resilience was like the neem tree - sturdy and unwavering. His mother's quiet strength was the cool shade beneath it, and his own curiosity was the restless breeze that rustled the leaves.

Even then, Narayan knew that life wouldn't always be kind. But he believed that with knowledge, courage, and the unwavering support of his family, he could face whatever lay ahead.

And in those moments of childhood wonder and quiet determination, the seeds of the man he would become were planted.

Lessons of Innocence

The sun hung low in the sky as Narayan walked through the bustling lanes of Sukhpura's market, a cloth bag swinging from his hand. The narrow streets were alive with colour and sound - vendors calling out their prices, women haggling over vegetables, and the scent of fresh produce mingling with the dusty air.

His mother had sent him out to buy vegetables for dinner, a task he took seriously. He mentally ticked off his list: potatoes, onions, tomatoes. Each item was carefully selected, weighed, and tucked into his bag.

As he was about to turn back, a gleaming stack of watermelons piled high on a cart caught his eye. The green-striped fruits looked so fresh, so inviting. His mouth watered at the thought of their sweet, cool juice sliding down his throat. It had been months since he'd last tasted watermelon, and the heat of the day made the idea even more tempting.

Narayan hesitated, then walked up to the vendor - a man in his forties with a kind smile and a neatly wrapped white turban.

"Bhaiya, yeh tarbooz kitne ka hai?" Narayan asked, his voice filled with curiosity.

The vendor replied, ***"Saath rupaye kilo."***

Narayan's eyes widened. He thought he heard *"sath rupaye"* instead of *"saath rupaye"* - not 7 rupaye, but **60 rupaye per kilogram**! He gulped, suddenly aware of how expensive the fruit seemed.

"Aur agar do lene hain toh?" he asked cautiously. What if two watermelons cost him a small fortune?

The vendor chuckled, picking up two watermelons and placing them on the old-fashioned weighing scale. The metal plates tipped back and forth before finally settling at **4.5 kilograms**.

"Kitna hua?" Narayan asked nervously, mentally calculating. If it was **60 rupaye per kilogram**, then **4.5 kilograms** would cost... He did the math quickly.

270 rupaye! His stomach dropped. That was too much! He imagined his mother's frown and his father's quiet disappointment. How could he justify spending so much on just watermelons?

The vendor smiled, a glint of amusement in his eyes. *"Bhaiya, poore 32 rupaye hue."*

Narayan blinked, confused. *"Sirf 32 rupaye?"*

"Yes, *beta*. It's just **7 rupees per kilogram**. Two watermelons for **32 rupaye**," the vendor said, his eyes twinkling.

Relief washed over Narayan's face, and his cheeks flushed red. He realised his mistake and felt a mix of embarrassment and amusement.

"Oh! Please give them to me,"

The vendor chuckled, carefully placing the watermelons in his bag. "You're an honest boy. Always double-check your maths!"

Narayan smiled sheepishly, paid the money, and walked home, the watermelons adding a delightful weight to his bag.

The Laughter at Home

As he stepped into the house, his father looked up from his newspaper, and his mother emerged from the kitchen, wiping her hands on her sari.

"What did you get, beta?" his mother asked.

"Watermelons!" Narayan announced proudly, placing the bag on the table.

His father raised an eyebrow. "That's a treat! How much did they cost?"

Narayan grinned and launched into the story: confusion over the price, his panic at the thought of spending 270 rupees, and the vendor's amused correction.

As he finished, his parents burst out laughing. His mother's laughter was like a bell, ringing through the room, while his father's deep chuckles shook his shoulders.

"Beta, 60 rupees for a kilo of watermelon? You thought you were buying gold!" his father said, wiping tears from his eyes.

Narayan blushed but couldn't help laughing along. The joy on their faces and the simplicity of the moment filled the room with warmth.

A Lesson in Simplicity

The next afternoon, they cut open the watermelons. The juice ran down the knife, bright and red, a perfect summer treat. With each sweet bite, Narayan savoured more than just the fruit. He cherished the laughter, the innocence, and the comforting presence of his family.

In the evening, they sat together on the veranda, the setting sun painting the sky in hues of orange and pink.

His father ruffled his hair. "Remember, Narayan, life is about small joys and simple moments. Never lose this innocence."

Narayan smiled; a seed of understanding planted in his heart. He knew he would carry this memory with him, a reminder that sometimes, the simplest mistakes can lead to the sweetest laughter.

And as the stars began to dot the night sky, the sound of their laughter lingered – a melody of love, warmth, and childhood innocence.

The Last in Line

The sun beat down on the school grounds, its heat shimmering off the dusty earth. Nervous tension clung to the air, palpable among the clusters of students waiting for their report cards. This was no ordinary day - it was the day of the 12th standard results, the final verdict before Narayan embarked on a new journey.

Narayan and his father, **Vijaynath,** stood quietly at the end of the line - their familiar spot, where life seemed to move at a gentler pace. Vijaynath's firm hand on Narayan's shoulder offered silent reassurance. The significance of this moment weighed heavier than any they had faced before, with each of Narayan's results carrying its own gravity.

Narayan's heart pounded. The paper he was about to receive held more than just marks; it held the key to his future. College, a world beyond the fields of Sukhpura, and the dreams his father had nurtured for him – all of it hinged on what lay within that folded sheet.

His father's voice was calm yet edged with anticipation. "Beta, whatever happens, we'll face it together."

Narayan nodded, swallowing the lump in his throat. This was more than just a result; it was the doorway to a new life.

As the line inched forward, Narayan whispered a silent prayer: *"Please, God. No more than three red lines. You've helped me through the last 12 years; just one more time, please!"* The red lines indicated the subjects he had failed. Four or more would mean repeating the year, shattering his dream of attending college. The mere thought of his father's disappointment was more than he could bear.

That day, standing at the back of the line, Narayan learned that survival sometimes came down to a single act of grace – a lesson that life would teach him again and again.

Three Red Lines of Fate

Finally, it was Narayan's turn. The teacher handed him the thin sheet of paper, its rustle sounding louder than it should have. Narayan's hands trembled as he unfolded the report card. His eyes darted over the marks, and his breath caught in his throat.

There they were – the dreaded red lines. One. Two. Three.

He blinked; his vision blurring slightly. He counted again. Just three red lines. No more, no less.

Relief flooded his body, so overwhelming that his knees nearly buckled. He exhaled a shaky breath, and his silent prayer was answered.

"Papa, three red lines," Narayan whispered in a voice, a mix of disbelief and gratitude. "I made it."

Vijaynath took the report card and scanned it carefully. A small, tired smile tugged at his lips. "You got grace marks in some subjects, Narayan. But you passed. That's what matters."

Narayan nodded, tears prickling his eyes. He knew the grace marks were just that - a gift, a lifeline extended by fate. He hadn't aced his exams, but he had crossed the line, however thin it might have been.

A Quiet Gratitude

They walked home together, Narayan clutching the report card like a fragile treasure. The weight of failure had lifted, replaced by a determination to do better.

As they reached the small gate of their home, Narayan looked up at the sky. The setting sun painted the horizon in hues of orange and purple.

"Thank you, God," he whispered. "I won't waste this chance."

His father squeezed his shoulder gently. "It's not always about how you start, *beta*. It's about how you keep going. This is just one step. There are many more ahead."

Narayan nodded. He knew this wasn't the end of his struggle, but for now, he was grateful for the chance to keep moving forward.

And as they stepped inside, the quiet walls of their home seemed to echo the unspoken promise between them: to rise, no matter how many times they stumbled.

Part 2: Seeds of Sacrifice

The sun stretched long shadows across the fields of Sukhpura as Narayan and his father settled on their old wooden bench outside their home. The breeze of dusk swayed the neem leaves, and the smell of freshly tilled soil lingered in the air.

His father, Vijaynath, was a man of few words but deep thoughts. His weathered face, lined with years of toil, was set in quiet determination. That evening, his eyes held a glimmer of resolve that Narayan couldn't quite understand yet.

"*Beta*, you've done well in school," Vijaynath began, his voice steady. "You have a chance to go to college in the city. It's time to think beyond this village."

Narayan's heart skipped a beat. The idea of leaving home, of venturing into the world beyond the familiar fields and dusty lanes, filled him with excitement and fear.

"But, Papa... the fees... how will we manage?" Narayan's voice trembled with worry. He knew the family's finances were tight. Every rupee mattered.

Vijaynath took a deep breath, his gaze fixed on the horizon. "I've thought about it. I'll sell a part of our land and use some of our savings. This is an investment in your future, Narayan. The land can give us crops, but your education can give us a new life."

Narayan's eyes widened. The land was their lifeline, their security. Selling even a part of it was a risk, a sacrifice that weighed heavily on his father's shoulders.

"But, Papa, what if..."

Vijaynath held up his hand, his eyes filled with unwavering conviction. "There's no 'what if.' I believe in you. You have a chance to do something we never dreamed of. I won't let you miss it because of fear."

He paused, his voice softening. "I've spent my life working these fields, Narayan, and I'm proud of it. But I want more for you. I want you to walk into a world where your mind and knowledge are your tools. I want you to live a life of confidence and fulfilment."

Narayan's eyes stung. His father's quiet resolve spoke louder than words - their land was just earth, but his future was hope. This was more than a financial decision - it was an act of faith, love, and hope.

"I won't let you down, *Papa*," Narayan whispered, his voice thick with emotion.

His father smiled, a rare softness breaking through his stern features. "I know you won't. Remember, knowledge is the one thing no one can take away from you. Carry it proudly."

The Weight of a Decision

The following day, Vijaynath finalised the sale of a small piece of their land. The money, though modest, was enough to cover Narayan's college fees and basic expenses in the city. As he handed over the cash, his hands trembled slightly, but his eyes shone with purpose.

When the day came for Narayan to leave for college, the entire village gathered to see him off. His father stood tall, pride and hope etched into his face. He placed a hand on Narayan's shoulder.

"Go, my son. Make your motherland proud. This is not just your journey; it is ours, too."

As the bus pulled away, Narayan looked back at his father, standing resolute, the fields behind him waving gently in the morning breeze. As he thought of his father's sacrifices and his mother's quiet strength, Narayan realised that the roots of his resilience ran deep. They had carried him through storms before, and they would take him through this one, too.

Narayan knew that this decision wasn't just about education. It was a bold step towards transforming his family's future and the society around him. And he vowed to honour that step, no matter how difficult the road ahead.

As the bus carried him away, he whispered to himself, *"This is just the beginning, and I'm ready for it."* The city awaited, full of unknowns, but he was ready to carry his roots forward.

* * * * *

Chapter 4

College and Friendship

Leaving Sukhpura felt like shedding a protective layer, but Narayan carried his roots with him. The resilience of his childhood and the quiet lessons under the neem tree whispered to him as he stepped through the gates of **Ichapuri College and University** in the bustling city of **Brahpura**. It was a world apart from the quiet simplicity of Sukhpura. The streets buzzed with life - rickshaws weaving, voices merging into a restless hum.

Narayan stood at the gates of **Ichapuri University**, his heart beating with a mixture of excitement and apprehension. He adjusted his backpack, took a deep breath, and walked through the gate. The campus sprawled before him - a maze of brick buildings, green lawns, and clusters of students who seemed to know exactly where they were going. Narayan felt small, a solitary figure amidst a sea of strangers.

As he walked through the gates, he reminded himself of the lessons from Sukhpura – the resilience his father taught him, the quiet strength he discovered under the neem tree. These memories steadied his nerves. He heard his father's voice in his mind: *"This is your journey, Narayan. Trust yourself, and trust the path ahead."*

There was no turning back. This was his chance to shape his future, to learn, to grow. His father's words echoed in his mind: *"Knowledge is your strongest weapon. Use it wisely."*

Forging New Bonds

Narayan found his rhythm, guided by the quiet confidence he'd built in Sukhpura. His earnest nature and thoughtful demeanour caught the attention of two students who would soon become his closest friends - **Shiv** and **Shreedhar**. In their laughter and debates, he discovered a camaraderie that echoed the warmth of his childhood friendships.

Shiv was a tall, lanky boy with a mischievous grin and a never-ending supply of jokes. Shreedhar, shorter and stockier, was the calm voice of reason who often pulled Shiv back from the brink of trouble.

The three of them were an unlikely trio, but their bond was instant and solid. They spent hours between classes under the old peepal tree, debating everything from politics to cricket scores.

"Narayan, you talk like an old man," Shiv teased one afternoon. "Don't you ever think about anything other than studies?"

Narayan laughed, shaking his head. "Someone has to keep you two grounded."

The Earnest *Hawabaaz*

Narayan soon earned the nickname **"*hawabaaz*"** - the boaster. He wasn't one to show off, but his passion for learning often made him sound like he knew everything. He took it in stride, knowing his friends meant no harm.

One afternoon, during a heated debate on economics, Narayan found himself surrounded by curious classmates. He spoke confidently, quoting theories and examples he'd read in newspapers and textbooks.

"Where do you get all this from, Narayan?" Shreedhar asked, impressed.

"From listening, reading, and sometimes," Narayan smirked, "just making sense of the chaos."

The crowd burst into laughter, and for the first time, Narayan felt a surge of belonging. He wasn't just a shy boy from a village; he was someone who could hold his own, someone who mattered.

Meeting Angelina

It was during one of these impromptu debates that Narayan first noticed **Angelina**. Her sharp gaze and quiet confidence reminded him of the banyan tree back home - strong, steady, and full of stories. He felt the stirrings of something familiar yet new, a connection that promised both challenge and growth.

There was something about her - a quiet strength that drew him in, even if he couldn't explain why. She stood at the back of the crowd, her arms crossed, a faint smile playing on her lips. Her dark eyes sparkled with curiosity and intelligence.

When the group dispersed, she walked up to him.

"You sure talk a lot," she teased, a playful glint in her eyes. "Ever wonder if you're making sense?"

Narayan blinked, momentarily stunned. "I - I try to," he stammered, his face flushing.

She laughed, a sound like wind chimes. "I need help with commerce. You seem to know your stuff. Think you can spare some time?"

Narayan nodded, too surprised to speak. He watched as she walked away, her confidence radiating like sunlight.

Late-Night Conversations

Their study sessions began the next day, the air between them tinged with cautious curiosity. At first, Narayan explained concepts, and Angelina asked sharp, insightful questions. But as days melted into weeks, the boundaries blurred. One afternoon, as they pored over finance notes, Narayan hesitated.

"Do you ever feel like... you're meant for something more?" he asked, his voice soft.

Angelina looked up, her eyes meeting his. "All the time," she whispered.

The quiet understanding that passed between them felt like a bridge to something deeper. They began to share not just academic ideas but fragments of their pasts and visions of the future. In those moments, the world outside their shared silence faded away. Narayan found himself looking forward to these meetings, his heart beating a little faster each time he saw her.

Late at night, they spoke on the phone, their voices hushed to avoid disturbing anyone around or waking anyone at Angelina's home.

"Do you ever wonder where we'll be in ten years?" she asked one night.

"All the time," Narayan admitted. "I want to do something meaningful. Build a life I can be proud of."

"Me too," she said softly. "I want to climb the corporate ladder, but sometimes I wonder if it's worth it. What if we lose ourselves along the way?"

"You won't," he assured her. "You're too strong for that."

She fell silent for a moment. "Maybe," she whispered. "And maybe that's why I need someone like you."

Narayan's heart soared, but he kept his voice steady. "I'll always be here."

The First Stirrings of Love

Their friendship deepened, a quiet undercurrent of something more beginning to flow between them. Narayan found himself thinking of her at odd moments - during lectures, while walking to class, and even as he drifted off to sleep.

One evening, as they sat on the steps of the library, Angelina turned to him.

"You know, you're not as much of a 'hawabaaz' as people say."

He smiled. "And you're not as intimidating as you pretend to be."

She laughed, but there was a softness in her eyes. The sun slipped below the horizon, draping the campus in a warm embrace of amber and deepening purple. For a moment, the world held its breath.

Narayan wanted to say something - to tell her what his heart was whispering - but fear held him back. Instead, he simply sat beside her, the unspoken words hanging between them like a fragile thread.

A New Chapter of Growth

College life was shaping him in ways he hadn't expected. His friendships with Shiv and Shreedhar gave him laughter and camaraderie. His connection with Angelina gave him hope and a glimpse of something beautiful.

But beneath the joy, a small voice warned him that life was rarely straightforward. Love, dreams, and expectations were threads in a complicated tapestry. For now, though, he was content to let the story unfold, one chapter at a time.

Narayan's college life was filled with laughter, and late-night study sessions were shared with Shiv and Shreedhar. The trio's debates under the peepal tree became a cherished routine. In these moments, Narayan felt a deep sense of belonging, a comfort that balanced the challenges of academic life.

But amidst the chaos of college life, there was one person who stood out - **Angelina**.

What began as study sessions soon evolved into something more. Their conversations flowed effortlessly from commerce theories to their dreams for the future. Narayan found comfort in her presence; her laughter was a melody that lingered in his mind long after they parted. And somewhere in those shared moments, he realised he was falling in love.

A Playful Exchange

One afternoon, while strolling through the campus together, Narayan and Angelina's conversation turned playful.

"You're such an idiot," Angelina teased, her eyes dancing with mischief. "Tell me, why do people in the West have red cheeks?"

Narayan grinned. "Simple, because of the winter."

She rolled her eyes. "You are an idiot. Their cheeks are red because they kiss each other on the cheeks. And see, you don't even kiss me."

Narayan laughed. "Well, I want to kiss you on your lips."

She arched an eyebrow, feigning mock outrage. "Hey, I wasn't asking for anything inappropriate. So, are we heading home today or what? Or are you planning to keep me here, listening to you all day? Not that I mind - I love hearing you talk."

Narayan smiled. "Tell me what I should do. Let's stay back at the college today, and we'll have the whole time to ourselves."

She shook her head, laughing. "Now you're going mad. I'm leaving for the day, and if you're interested in coming down with me, then please pick up your bag and those thick books of yours that you always carry."

Bridges Across Miles

The evening air was still, the sky painted in hues of fading orange as Narayan sat by the small wooden desk in his modest college dorm room. The weight of the recent exams, the anxiety over his results, and his desire not to disappoint his father pressed heavily on his shoulders.

With a deep breath, he picked up his pen and a sheet of paper. His fingers trembled slightly as he began to write.

A Letter of Confession

Dearest Papa,

I hope this letter finds you in good health. I miss home more than I can say. The warmth of our village, the comfort of our home, and your steady words of encouragement seem so far away now.

I want to tell you that my exams were harder than I expected. I tried my best, but I'm afraid I might not have done well in all the subjects. The fear of failure sits heavily on my mind. I keep thinking of your sacrifices and how you sold a piece of our land to send me here. I don't want to let you down.

Please forgive me if I haven't lived up to your expectations. I promise I will work harder. I just need to hear from you, Papa, to know that you still believe in me, no matter what.

Your loving son,
Narayan

Narayan folded the letter carefully and slipped it into an envelope. As he wrote his father's name and the address of Sukhpura, he felt a surge of comfort. No matter how far he travelled, these words were a bridge to his roots, a reminder that the strength of home was never out of reach.

He made his way to the nearby post office as the sun slipped beneath the horizon, painting the streets with deep, elongated shadows. The red and white of the post office sign glowed faintly under the streetlights. A postal worker in a crisp khaki uniform nodded to him with a smile.

"Posting a letter home, beta?" the man asked kindly.

Narayan nodded. "Yes, to my father."

The worker took the letter, stamping it with practised efficiency. "Don't worry. With the new systems we have now, it will be in your father's hands in one day."

Narayan felt a flutter of hope. The thought that his words would reach his father so quickly was a comfort he hadn't expected. He thanked the postal worker and walked back to his dorm, feeling lighter.

A Swift Reply

Two days later, just after his last lecture, Narayan returned to his room to find a letter on his desk, the familiar handwriting of his father making his heart leap. He tore open the envelope with trembling fingers.

Dearest Narayan,

I received your letter, and I felt your worry in every word. You must remember, my son, that your journey is not measured by one exam or one result. What matters is that you keep trying and learning.

Don't let the fear of failure hold you back. You have already made me proud by daring to dream beyond this village. Whatever happens, know that I believe in you and always will.

You are not alone. Every time you take a step forward, your mother and I are with you. Trust yourself and trust that your hard work will bear fruit.

Write to me anytime, and remember, these letters keep us connected even when we're miles apart. Thanks to the fast-moving hands of the post office, my words can reach you as quickly as my thoughts.

Stay strong, beta.

Your loving,
Papa

The Power of Connection

Narayan clutched the letter to his chest, tears pricking his eyes. His father's words, carried swiftly across miles, wrapped around him like a warm embrace. The fear and doubt that had clouded his mind began to lift.

He marvelled at the simple yet profound efficiency of the modernised postal system - a bridge between his world of uncertainty and the unwavering support of home. Even in a world moving faster every day, these letters felt like anchors, keeping his spirit grounded.

Narayan smiled softly. He had his father's belief, and that was enough to keep him going.

A New Resolve

The weight of his college exams lifted, and Narayan felt a blend of relief and quiet resolve. He glanced at his average exam results, his fingers tightening around the paper. His shoulders loosened just a fraction, and a breath he didn't know he'd been holding slipped out. He folded the sheet carefully and slipped it into his bag, his jaw set in a firm line.

The echo of footsteps and chatter around him faded as he walked towards the campus gate, his eyes fixed on the horizon. He clenched his fists briefly, then relaxed them - a silent promise forming in his mind. He wouldn't let this chance slip away again.

When news of the **National Simulation Management Games** reached him, he straightened; his eyes narrowed with focus. The world around him sharpened.

It was time to move forward.

Triumph Through Trust

The sun filtered through the windows of **Ichapuri University's** library, casting a warm glow over rows of books and bustling students. Narayan sat at a table with his nose buried in a management textbook, his mind whirling with strategies and scenarios. The upcoming **National Simulation Management Games** were all he could think about.

The competition was designed to test participants' strategic thinking, problem-solving skills, and ability to manage simulated business environments under pressure. Winning it was a matter of pride, a testament to one's ability to thrive in challenging situations.

His friend Shiv plopped down next to him, with a mischievous grin on his face.

"Are you still over-preparing for this, *hawabaaz*?" Shiv teased. "You know it's just a game."

"It's not just a game, Shiv," Narayan replied, his eyes shining with determination. "It's an opportunity. Winning this could give us recognition and open doors for the future."

From across the table, Shreedhar nodded in agreement. "Narayan's right. This is our chance to prove we can handle real-world challenges."

A voice chimed in from behind them. "Then let's make it count."

They turned to see Angelina, her eyes sharp with confidence and a smile playing on her lips.

"I'm in. Let's form a team and give this everything we've got."

Narayan's heart swelled. With Shiv's creativity, Shreedhar's pragmatism, Angelina's strategic insight, and his own analytical skills, they had a well-rounded team of four. The thought of working together ignited a spark of excitement.

Forming the Dream Team

The next few weeks were a whirlwind of preparation. The team met in classrooms, coffee shops, and dorm rooms, refining their strategies, discussing market scenarios, and simulating decision-making under pressure. They pored over case studies, debated approaches, and tackled mock simulations – each session making them sharper and more cohesive.

Their bond grew stronger. They trusted each other's skills and instincts, and that trust became the foundation of their teamwork.

Narayan often reminded them, "No matter what happens, we stick together. We trust each other's decisions and keep moving forward."

The afternoon before the competition, they gathered for one final strategy session. As they reviewed their plans, Shiv leaned back and sighed dramatically.

"Win or lose, at least we'll have a good story to tell."

Angelina smirked. "We're not losing, Shiv. We've worked too hard for that."

Shreedhar smiled. "She's right. We've got this."

Narayan looked around the room at his teammates, a surge of gratitude filling his chest. They were more than just friends now - they were a unit, bound by trust and determination.

The Battle Begins

The venue for the **National Simulation Management Games** buzzed with energy. Teams from top universities and colleges filled the hall, their faces a mix of excitement and nerves. The competition was fierce, with participants who were as determined and skilled as Narayan's team.

The simulation began. Each team was given control of a virtual company, tasked with making critical decisions in production, marketing, finance, and human resources. Each round represented a fiscal quarter, and the goal was to maximise profits, growth, and customer satisfaction.

Narayan's team huddled together, eyes glued to the screen.

"Alright," Narayan said, his voice steady. "Let's focus on our strengths. Angelina, lead on marketing strategies. Shreedhar, keep an eye on finances. Shiv, handle product development. I'll oversee the overall strategy and make sure we're aligned."

"Got it," they chorused.

The timer started, and the game was on.

Rising to the Challenge

The first few rounds were intense. Decisions had to be made quickly, with incomplete information and evolving market conditions. Some teams faltered under pressure, their strategies unravelling.

But Narayan's team stayed calm.

As the competition loomed, Narayan remembered his father's words: *"Trust the process, beta. Resilience is built in moments of doubt."* He took a deep breath and faced the challenge head-on.

They trusted each other's inputs, debated respectfully, and adapted to changes. When a sudden market shift threw their initial strategy off course, it was Angelina who suggested a pivot in marketing.

"Let's target a different demographic," she said confidently. "We can't compete on price, but we can dominate with quality."

Narayan nodded. "Let's do it."

Shiv adjusted the product features, and Shreedhar recalculated the budget. Their new strategy paid off - their virtual company's market share began to climb.

Other teams noticed their success. Whispers of admiration spread through the room. Narayan's team was not just surviving the simulation; they were thriving.

The Final Round

As they entered the final round, the top teams were neck and neck. The pressure mounted, but Narayan's team held their ground. In their debates and laughter, Narayan found echoes of his father's steady belief - that trust could weather any storm.

Their last decision was critical – a risky expansion into a new market. The room was tense as they analysed the risks.

"Do we go for it?" Shreedhar asked, his voice uncertain.

Narayan looked at his teammates, their faces filled with determination.

"Yes," Narayan said firmly. "We've come this far by trusting each other. Let's trust this decision."

They locked in their choice and waited.

The simulation ended. The results flashed on the screen.

Victory

A hush fell over the room as the scores were announced. When the name of their college was called as the **Zonal Champions**, the room erupted in applause.

Narayan's team jumped to their feet, joy and relief washing over them. They hugged each other, the weight of their hard work finally lifting.

"We did it!" Shiv shouted, his grin wider than ever.

Angelina's eyes sparkled. "I told you we weren't losing."

Shreedhar's usually calm face broke into a smile. "We trusted each other, and it paid off."

Narayan's heart swelled with pride and gratitude. This achievement was not just about the trophy - it was a reflection of trust, teamwork, and the power of standing side by side to reach a common goal. In his heart, he knew this victory wasn't just about the competition. It was a reflection of everything he'd learned - from the quiet fields of Sukhpura to the buzzing campus of Ichapuri. Trust, confidence, and resilience had carried him through, and they would continue to guide him, no matter the challenge.

A Lesson in Trust

As they stood on the stage, holding their trophy, Narayan reflected on the journey. They had faced challenges, doubts, and pressure, but they had overcome them together.

In his heart, he knew this victory wasn't just about the competition. It was about learning that trust, confidence, and collaboration could turn any challenge into a triumph.

In that moment of triumph, Narayan realised that the resilience his father had taught him wasn't just about facing failure – it was also about embracing trust and standing strong together.

His father's words echoed in his mind: *"True strength lies in trusting those around you."*.

He would carry this lesson with him for the rest of his life.

Whispers of Love in Motion – In an Auto-Rickshaw

Days passed, and soon the college placement season was about to begin. The realisation of his feelings grew heavier with each passing day. Opportunities favoured him, and he landed his first job offer as a Junior Analyst at a local consultancy firm. He felt a rush of excitement and purpose. He needed office clothes to match his new role, and with his father's support, he went shopping for warm shirts and trousers.

Angelina had accompanied him, teasing him over his indecisiveness.

"Do you think this tie will impress your clients?" she laughed, holding up a bright red one.

Narayan rolled his eyes. "I'm going for serious analyst vibes, not circus clown."

She grinned. "Suit yourself."

As the evening settled and the city lights flickered to life, they squeezed into an auto-rickshaw, their shopping bags piled at their feet. The rickshaw rattled forward, weaving through traffic, the air filled with the sharp tang of exhaust and the distant calls of street vendors.

Narayan's heart pounded. He could feel the weight of the moment pressing down on him, the words he wanted to say fighting to break free.

He glanced at Angelina, her face softly illuminated by the streetlights. Her hair fluttered in the breeze, and she seemed lost in thought, watching the world blur past. As he prepared to blurt out his feelings, a wave of memories washed over him - the quiet resilience of Sukhpura, the ache of unspoken words, the promise he'd made to himself never to hold back again. This wasn't just a confession but a step forward, a choice to embrace hope over fear.

He took a deep breath, his palms clammy.

"Angelina," he said, his voice barely rising above the engine's growl.

She turned to him, eyebrows raised. "Hmm?"

He hesitated, the noise of the rickshaw drowning out his thoughts. But the words tumbled out before he could stop them.

"I... I think I'm in love with you."

The rickshaw jolted over a pothole, and his words were swallowed by the clamour of the city. He wasn't even sure if she had heard him. His face flushed with embarrassment.

As the words left his lips, Narayan felt a flutter of uncertainty. He'd always been cautious with his heart, careful not to let his feelings get the better of him. But with Angelina, it felt different. This wasn't a reckless leap; it was a chance he was willing to take, a step towards something that felt real and right.

Angelina blinked at him, surprise flickering across her face. And then, to his astonishment, she burst out laughing – a bright, genuine laugh that rang out above the din.

"Did you just propose to me in an auto-rickshaw?" she asked, her eyes shining with amusement.

His stomach twisted. "I - I didn't plan it. I'm sorry. Maybe I shouldn't have said anything."

She shook her head, still chuckling. "You're unbelievable, Narayan."

The journey continued, wrapped in an unspoken stillness. Her laughter faded, replaced by a thoughtful quiet. She looked out the window, the city lights reflecting in her eyes. Narayan's heart sank. *I've ruined everything,* he thought. *I shouldn't have risked our friendship.*

When they reached her home, she stepped out of the rickshaw, gave him a small wave, and disappeared inside without saying another word.

Beneath the quiet of the night, he lay staring at the ceiling, lost in a storm of thoughts. His mind raced with regret. He checked his phone repeatedly, hoping for a message that didn't come. The emptiness of the night stretched on, each minute a reminder of what he feared he'd lost.

A New Morning

The first rays of dawn crept through his window. Just as he was about to give up hope, his phone buzzed.

He grabbed it, his heart in his throat.

Angelina: *"Good morning, Narayan. You're an idiot, but I think you're my kind of idiot. Let's talk."*

A slow smile spread across his face. Relief and joy bubbled up inside him, washing away the fear from the night before.

He typed back, his fingers steady.

Narayan: *"I'm ready when you are."*

In the camaraderie of Shiv and Shreedhar and the quiet connection with Angelina, Narayan found pieces of the home he'd left behind. Yet, he didn't know that love, once so full of promise, could still slip through his fingers, leaving him once again to draw on the strength of his roots.

* * * * *

Chapter 5

Love and Challenges

Over the months, Narayan's bond with Angelina deepened. Their study sessions evolved into heartfelt conversations and quiet moments of connection. The warmth of her smile and the comfort of their shared dreams brought a new light into his world.

Narayan marvelled at how naturally Angelina had become part of his life. Her presence was a quiet melody, threading through the routine of his thoughts. With her, he felt seen and understood in ways he hadn't thought possible.

For Angelina, Narayan was a steady anchor in a world that often felt chaotic. His sincerity, his unwavering belief in her dreams, and his quiet strength grounded her.

Despite the whispers, their love continued to bloom, finding joy in the quiet moments they shared.

Moments of Joy

One crisp winter morning, they skipped a lecture and wandered through the gardens behind the college. The dew sparkled on the grass, and the flowers bloomed with a vibrant defiance against the chill.

Angelina stopped to admire a marigold, its orange petals glowing in the sunlight.

"It's beautiful," she said softly.

Narayan smiled, his gaze fixed on her. "Yes, it is,"

She caught his eye and blushed. "You're terrible at being subtle."

"Maybe I don't want to be subtle," he replied, his voice low.

She took his hand, her fingers threading through his. "I'm glad you're not."

They stood there, time suspended, the world reduced to the warmth of their hands and the steady rhythm of their hearts.

Whispers and Shadows

But love, no matter how pure, does not exist in a vacuum. Whispers of their relationship rippled through the college. Curious glances turned into judgemental stares, and unspoken questions lingered like shadows.

One afternoon, Shiv pulled Narayan aside, concern etched on his face.

"Narayan, people are talking. They say Angelina's family won't accept someone like you."

Narayan's jaw tightened. "What do you mean, 'someone like me'?"

Shiv hesitated. "You know what I mean. Her family is wealthy and modern. They won't understand someone from a small village, no matter how smart or kind you are."

Narayan's heart clenched. He knew Shiv wasn't trying to hurt him; he was just voicing the reality Narayan had tried to ignore.

"Angelina loves me," Narayan said firmly. "We'll figure it out."

But the seed of doubt had been planted, gnawing at the edges of his confidence. Narayan walked away from Shiv, the words echoing in his mind. He had climbed so many walls already - could he really break this one?

The Weight of Expectations

One crisp afternoon, as they walked through the campus gardens, Angelina paused by a flower bed.

"My parents always wanted me to marry someone... established," she said, her voice distant. "Someone who fits their world."

Narayan's heart tightened, but he smiled. "I may not fit their mould, but I can build a world for us."

She smiled back, but the worry in her eyes lingered like a shadow neither of them wanted to acknowledge.

The first crack appeared during a phone call one evening. Narayan had just finished his assignments when his phone buzzed.

"Hey, Narayan," Angelina's voice was strained. "Can we talk?"

"Of course. What's wrong?"

She took a deep breath. "My parents found out about us. They're not happy. They think... they think you're not the right match for me."

Her words hit him like a punch to the gut, but beneath the shock, a creeping fear surfaced - had he always known this was coming? He clenched his fists, fighting the tremor in his voice.

"And what do you think?"

She turned away, her gaze fixed on the horizon. "I love you, Narayan. But every night, I hear my parents' voices, their expectations like a weight I can't shake off. I want to fight for us, but... sometimes, I wonder if love is enough to carry that burden."

The hesitation in her eyes mirrored the doubt gnawing at his heart.

"Angelina, we can make this work. Love matters more than anything."

"It's not that simple," she whispered. "They expect so much from me. I don't want to let them down."

His chest felt tight. "So, what are you saying?"

"I don't know," she said, tears in her voice. "I need time to think."

The line went silent. Narayan felt as though the ground had been ripped out from under him.

Struggle and Reflection

In the days that followed, Narayan wrestled with his thoughts. He replayed their conversations, searching for answers, for hope. The village boy who once believed that love could conquer anything now faced the harsh reality of societal expectations.

His father's words echoed in his mind: *Life is full of battles, son. Some you win, some you lose. What matters is that you stay true to yourself.*

But what did staying true mean now? Was it holding onto his love or letting it go for her happiness?

A Moment of Resolve

One afternoon, under a sky thick with clouds, Narayan sat on the steps of the library, his head buried in his hands. The weight of uncertainty pressed against his chest. Above him, the sky blazed with hues of red and gold, reflecting the turmoil inside.

A gentle touch on his shoulder broke his spiral of thoughts. He looked up to see Angelina standing there, her eyes glistening with tears.

"Narayan," she whispered, her voice trembling, "I'm scared. I don't want to lose you."

He rose to his feet, taking her hands in his. Her fingers were cold, but her touch was familiar.

"We'll fight this together," he said, his voice steady. "No matter what happens, I'm with you."

A tear slipped down her cheek. "I want to believe that."

"Then believe it," he urged softly. "We'll figure this out, one step at a time."

They held each other tightly, their embrace a fragile shield against the world. Their resolve flickered like a candle in the wind, glowing with hope but threatened by an unseen storm. The unease gnawed at the back of Narayan's mind - a shadow of what was yet to come.

As they turned to leave, the clouds opened. The rain poured down, soaking them within seconds. Instinctively, Narayan reached for his bag to shield himself, but Angelina grabbed his hand and pulled him into the open street.

"Come on!" she laughed, the sound strained but bright, her eyes sparkling. "You can't hide from it."

Before he could protest, she twirled, her arms spread wide, her face tilted to the sky. Raindrops traced her cheeks like glistening jewels. For a moment, her laughter was genuine, a fleeting defiance of the fears consuming them.

Narayan's lips curled into a hesitant smile. He took a deep breath and stepped into the storm, the cold rain shocking his skin. They spun together, water streaming off their hair and clothes, the world around them dissolving into a blur of grey.

The rain muffled the city's noise as if creating a sanctuary just for them. In that downpour, there were no whispered doubts, no expectations - just the reckless joy of being together. Narayan caught her hand and pulled her close, their laughter mingling with the drumming rain.

For a fleeting second, their eyes met, and everything felt right. The storm washed away their fears, if only briefly. The rain could not erase the shadows between them, but in that moment, they chose to believe it could.

As the rain continued to fall, Narayan held onto the illusion a little longer, even as he felt it slipping through his fingers like water.

* * * * *

Chapter 6

Decisions and Consequences

Expectations weighed heavily on Narayan and Angelina. The burden grew with each passing day. The once effortless flow of their conversations slowed, and the laughter that had once bound them now felt strained, edged with doubt.

Narayan clung to the belief that love would overcome every obstacle. After all, hadn't they weathered so much already? The memories of their resolve to fight together still pulsed in his mind, but doubt, like a creeping vine, wrapped tighter around his heart.

The Breaking Point

The rainy afternoon mirrored the storm within him. The library, once their refuge, felt colder now, its familiar shelves shadowed with uncertainty. Narayan's heart sank as he saw Angelina, her eyes red-rimmed, the weight of sleepless nights etched across her face.

She took a shaky breath. "Narayan, we need to talk."

The air stilled, each word cutting deeper than he was prepared for.

Angelina's voice trembled. "I've spent nights arguing with my parents, trying to make them see us the way I do. But they won't listen, Narayan. They see our differences - our backgrounds, our futures - and they're scared for me."

Her eyes glistened with frustration. "I love you, but I'm caught between their expectations and my own heart. I feel like I'm losing myself."

Desperation clawed at him. "Angelina, we knew this wouldn't be easy. We promised to fight together."

She shook her head, tears streaming down her cheeks. "I'm exhausted, Narayan. Every conversation at home is a battle, every glance a reminder that I'm disappointing them. I lie awake at night, torn between you and the people who raised me. I love you - God, I love you - but love feels like a thread that's fraying under this weight."

Her voice cracked, and she looked at him with a desperation that mirrored his own. "I want to believe we can make it, but I'm scared the cost will be too high for both of us."

The finality in her words was a cold wind that blew through the spaces of his heart, extinguishing the hope he had clung to. The certainty he had leaned on crumbled. He searched her eyes, hoping for hesitation, for doubt. But all he found was pain - a reflection of his own.

"So, that's it?" he whispered. "After everything?"

Her sob was a quiet thunder. "I can't lose them, Narayan. I'm so sorry."

She reached for his hand, but he pulled away; the touch that once grounded him now a cruel reminder of loss. Her words felt like stones breaking the fragile bridge they had built together. Each syllable crumbled the future they had dared to dream.

"I hope you find happiness," he choked out, his voice breaking.

Without another word, she walked away, the sound of her footsteps dissolving into the rain. The rain pelted against the library windows, like tears falling from the banyan leaves in Sukhpura. Narayan sat motionless, the storm outside crashing against the windows, echoing the devastation within.

A World Without Colour

The days blurred into a grey monotony. Narayan moved through his life mechanically - attending lectures, answering questions, nodding at friends' words - all while his mind spiralled through memories of Angelina. The vibrant hues of their shared moments faded into shadows, the ache relentless. Each morning, he forced himself out of bed, the weight of emptiness pressing on his chest. The city outside continued its relentless march - cars honked, trains clattered, people hurried - but he felt disconnected from it all.

Shiv's voice was a faint comfort. "Give it time, Narayan. You'll heal."

But time felt like a cruel extension of pain, each second stretching the wound deeper.

He wondered if he was becoming a modern Devdas, lost in melancholy. The irony made him laugh bitterly. *Life is give and take,* he thought. *But what happens when you've given everything and are left empty-handed?*

Letter to His Father

In the suffocating quiet of his room, Narayan picked up a pen. Writing felt like the only way to release the storm in his heart.

Dearest Papa,

I've lost her. Angelina is gone, and with her, a part of me feels lost too. I did everything I could, but sometimes love isn't enough.

I feel like I've failed - not just her, but myself. The dreams we shared are ashes now.

How do I move forward, Papa? How do I believe in a future that feels so empty?

Your son,
Narayan

A Father's Wisdom

His father's reply came quickly, within the time he expected; his steady handwriting a beacon of comfort.

My Dear Narayan,

I know your pain, and I wish I could take it away. But sometimes, the greatest lessons come from the deepest wounds.

You feel like you've lost everything, but you haven't lost yourself. That is your greatest strength.

Life is full of choices. Angelina made hers. Maybe, just maybe, she might come back. Now you must make yours. Will you let this pain define you, or will you rise above it?

Resilience isn't about avoiding pain; it's about enduring it, learning from it, and moving forward.

This loss is part of your story but not the end of it. Trust that life has more for you.

I believe in you, always.
Papa

A New Resolve

Narayan read his father's words, each one seeping into his shattered heart. The pain didn't disappear, but a spark of determination flickered. He stood by the window, watching dawn break through the darkness.

The world was still turning, and maybe he could too.

He would rise. He would endure. And one day, he would turn this pain into purpose.

The Struggle and the Smoke

But resilience was not a straight path. The demands of his job as a Junior Analyst weighed heavily. Days blurred into relentless cycles of reports, deadlines, and silent grief. The pressure mounted and escaped whispered temptations.

One evening, after an exhausting 14-hour day, Narayan stood outside the office building, the cool night air brushing his face. His thoughts raced, a chaotic whirlwind of frustration, regret, and confusion.

His colleague, Nandu, leaned against the wall, a cigarette dangling between his fingers. The faint glow of the ember pulsed like a heartbeat.

"Rough day?" Nandu asked, exhaling a cloud of smoke.

Narayan nodded, his shoulders slumping. "Feels like they all are."

Nandu held out a cigarette. "Try this. It helps, at least for a moment."

Narayan hesitated. He remembered his father's stern warnings about smoking and the lectures about health and discipline. But tonight, those memories felt distant. He craved an escape, a moment of numbness.

He took the cigarette, lit it, and inhaled. The smoke burned his throat, making him cough, but the sensation distracted him from the storm in his mind. The next drag was easier, the bitterness settling into a strange calm.

For the first time in weeks, his thoughts quietened - even if only for a few minutes.

The Spiral

But what started as a crutch became a chain. Narayan drifted deeper, the smoke a veil over his reality. A cigarette during breaks, another after lunch, and one more on the way home. Each puff felt like a small rebellion against the chaos, a momentary pause button on his problems.

Shiv and Shreedhar noticed the change.

"You're smoking a lot these days," Shiv said, concern in his voice. "Are you okay?"

Narayan shrugged. "It helps me think."

But deep down, he knew he was losing control. The smoke filled the gaps where his confidence used to be. He hated the smell that clung to his clothes, the bitter taste on his tongue. Yet, he couldn't stop.

A Harsh Wake-Up Call

One Saturday morning, Narayan received a call from Shreedhar.

"Hey, Narayan," Shreedhar's voice was thick with grief. "My dad… he passed away last night. Heart attack. The doctors said years of smoking made it worse."

The words struck Narayan like a physical blow. He remembered Shreedhar's father - a kind man with a booming laugh and eyes that twinkled with mischief. Gone, just like that.

Narayan hung up the phone, his hands trembling. He looked at the half-empty pack of cigarettes on his desk. The realisation crashed over him: *This is where I'm headed if I don't stop.*

He thought of his father, the sacrifices he made, and the dreams he had for his son. He thought of Angelina and how disappointed she would be if she saw him like this. And he thought of himself - the boy who once believed he could conquer anything with sheer willpower.

Breaking Free

Shreedhar's loss was the wake-up call Narayan needed - a stark reminder of the dangers of destructive paths. He tossed the pack of cigarettes into a trash bin near the lake. As he stood there, he watched the gentle ripples on the water's surface, feeling his frustration and regret slowly begin to dissipate.

He took a breath - a clean, deliberate breath - filling his lungs with air untainted by smoke. The craving whispered, but his resolve roared louder.

He was done hiding behind the smoke. He was ready to breathe, to rebuild, to rise.

"When the stars are low,
When the night is dark,
I look for my flow."

I seek a strength that is deep within me,
I look for a moment when I can break free.

I wait for the day when I can stand against the sun,
I pray for the day when I can know myself."

Closing Connection

Narayan wandered through the campus, his footsteps echoing in the deserted corridor. He found himself standing outside the library - the place where they first met. He could almost see her there, standing at the back with her arms crossed, that knowing smile playing on her lips.

He walked to the gardens behind the college, where they used to sit, hands intertwined, talking about futures they thought they'd share. The marigolds still bloomed, bright and defiant against the cool breeze. He crouched down, brushing his fingers over the petals, remembering how she once called them "little suns."

His chest ached with the memory of her laughter - a sound now buried under the silence she'd left behind. He closed his eyes and whispered a fragment of a promise they once made: "We'll figure it out together."

But the emptiness around him whispered its cold reply. He was alone, and its weight pressed down harder than ever.

Yet, as he rose, a flicker of strength ignited within him - fragile but undeniable. The places they'd shared remained, but he had changed. He could grieve and still move forward - that was resilience. He inhaled deeply, letting the sharp scent of marigolds fill his lungs, a reminder that life, no matter how battered, could bloom again.

Narayan's journey had been marked by love, loss, hope, and despair. But through it all, the lessons of his roots, his father's unwavering belief, and the resilience etched into his soul guided him forward. The road was still uncertain, but with each step, he moved towards the light.

This was not the end - merely another chapter in his story of hope, resilience, and the quiet strength to begin again. He took a deep breath, the memory of **Sukhpura's** neem tree steadying him. As the wind brushed his face, he knew the roots of his past would nourish his path forward, no matter how uncertain.

A New Dawn

Narayan stood at his window, the early dawn casting muted hues over the cityscape. The ache of loss still throbbed beneath the surface, but as he watched the world slowly wake, a thought crystallised: *Pain could either paralyse you or propel you forward.*

He inhaled deeply, the cool air bracing. *I've grieved enough. It's time to rebuild.*

The weight of his father's unwavering belief steadied him. There was still a future waiting, shaped not by what he had lost but by what he could still achieve. His path wasn't broken - just redirected.

* * * *

Chapter 7

A New Path

The world didn't stop for heartbreak. His father's letter comforted him. The last call from Angelina confirmed that she was no longer a part of his life. The sun continued to rise, and Narayan moved forward, one cautious step at a time. Determined to change his circumstances, he secured a position as a Junior Analyst at **Apirax Capital**, a mid-sized investment banking firm in **Mumbai**, far from **Brahpura**.

The office was a universe unto itself - gleaming glass walls, hushed conversations, and the relentless hum of ambition. Narayan's days were filled with numbers, reports, and tight deadlines. The rhythm of the corporate world was fast and unforgiving, but it offered something Narayan desperately needed: a chance to rebuild himself.

The Grind of an Analyst

Narayan quickly learned that investment banking was not for the faint-hearted. His days often stretched into nights, and weekends were no longer his own. He analysed market trends, prepared pitch books, and supported senior associates in closing deals. Every project was a test of endurance, precision, and resilience.

He thrived on the challenge, his mind sharp and focused. The analytical skills he had honed in college found purpose here, and his ability to see patterns and trends earned him quiet respect among his peers.

But the grind took its toll. The long hours and pressure to perform weighed on him. The city's relentless pace mirrored the pressure in his own mind – a constant reminder of everything he was trying to prove to himself and the world.

Late at night, in the empty office, he sometimes paused to look at the city lights. He wondered if this was what success felt like or if he was just running from the echoes of his past.

An Unexpected Opportunity

Six months into his job, Narayan's diligence paid off. One morning, his manager, Mr. Iyer, called him into his glass-walled office. Mr. Iyer was a seasoned banker with silver hair and eyes that missed nothing.

"Good work on the Sharma deal, Narayan," Mr. Iyer said, handing him a file. "Your analysis was thorough and timely. We need someone reliable to assist with a merger project for a European client. You'll be travelling to **London** for three weeks."

Narayan's heart leaped. *London.* The word held a promise of something new - a break from the monotony, a chance to see a world beyond his own.

"Thank you, sir," Narayan said, trying to keep his excitement in check. "I won't let you down."

"I know you won't," Mr. Iyer replied, a rare smile breaking through his stern demeanour. "Remember, every experience teaches you something. Be open to learning."

The London Dream

The day Narayan's ticket to London arrived, it felt like he was holding a piece of magic in his hands. The shiny paper with his name printed on it wasn't just a ticket; it was the culmination of years of hard work, sacrifice, and resilience. For a boy who grew up in the dusty lanes of Sukhpura, this was a moment of unimaginable pride.

"London," he whispered, the word brimming with excitement, fear, and endless possibility. Without hesitation, he booked a train to Sukhpura, determined to see his parents before embarking on this new journey.

A Family's Pride

His mother watched him from the doorway, her eyes glistening with tears. She stepped forward, placing a hand on his shoulder.

"Your dream is coming true, *beta*. You're the first in our family to go so far. Your father and I... we're so proud of you."

His father entered the room, his face a mixture of joy and quiet pride.

"Narayan, remember what I've always told you - wherever you go, carry our values and your integrity. That's what will make you stand tall."

Narayan nodded, swallowing the lump in his throat.

"I promise, Papa. I'll make you proud."

His father smiled. "You already have."

The next few days were a blur of preparations. His mother packed his clothes with loving care, folding each shirt meticulously as if each crease held a blessing. His father gave him final words of wisdom, reminding him to be cautious, to learn, and to embrace the experience fully.

On the day of his departure, the entire village gathered at the railway station. His mother's eyes glistened with tears, but a brave smile shone through them.

"Call us whenever you can," she said, her voice quivering.

"I will, Maa," Narayan promised.

As the train pulled away, he waved, his heart aching with the bittersweet pull of leaving home and the exhilaration of new adventures ahead.

The Flight of Dreams

Narayan's excitement thrummed steadily as he boarded the plane. He settled into his seat, eyes wide as he took in the rows of seats, blinking lights, and the distant roar of engines. When the plane finally took off, his stomach flipped with nervous anticipation. He watched the earth grow smaller beneath him, the fields and rivers of his homeland fading into a patchwork quilt.

He thought of his parents, their dreams interwoven with his own. This wasn't just his journey; it was theirs, too. Their sacrifices, encouragement, and belief had carried him to this moment. As the plane soared into the sky, he closed his eyes and whispered prayers to his forefathers.

First Impressions of London

Narayan's breath caught in his throat when the plane landed at Heathrow Airport. He stepped off the plane into a world he had only seen in movies and magazines. The air was crisp, the sky an endless grey, and the sheer scale of the airport left him in awe.

Everything felt foreign - the accents, the signs, the automated announcements. Yet, a thrill of excitement surged through him. He was here. He had made it.

A cab took him through the heart of London. The city unfolded before him like a grand tapestry: centuries-old buildings standing beside gleaming skyscrapers, the River Thames winding through the metropolis, and red double-decker buses weaving through traffic.

His eyes darted from one sight to the next. He marvelled at the London Eye, the towering presence of Big Ben, and the historic majesty of the Tower of London. Every street seemed to hum with stories, each corner alive with a vibrant pulse of life.

A New World

Narayan's first glimpse of London was through the window of a black cab - a city where glass skyscrapers and centuries-old architecture stood side by side. The grey sky seemed endless, and the air held a chill that woke him up more than any cup of coffee could.

The office of **KrestBnk International**, his client, was located in the heart of the financial district. The atmosphere was formal but less rigid than what he was used to. People walked with quiet confidence; their conversations were punctuated by a variety of accents.

On his second day, he met **Clairey Bennett**, a senior analyst assigned to guide him through the project. **Clairey** was in her early thirties, sharp-eyed, and effortlessly poised.

"Welcome to the grind, Narayan," she said with a wry smile. "But don't worry – we also know how to enjoy a good cup of tea here."

Her warmth put him at ease, and over the next few days, they worked seamlessly together. Clairey's approach to work was meticulous yet balanced. She encouraged questions and valued insights, no matter where they came from.

One afternoon, as they finalised a report, she leaned back in her chair and said, "You know, Narayan, you remind me of myself when I started. Always pushing, always trying to prove something."

Narayan looked up, surprised. "Isn't that what we're supposed to do?"

"To an extent," she said, her gaze thoughtful. "But remember, work isn't everything. Life is bigger than spreadsheets and deals. The trick is finding balance."

Her words stayed with him, an echo that grew louder each time he burned the midnight oil.

Exploring a New Experience

During the day, Narayan attended meetings and collaborated with colleagues at KrestBnk International. The sleek, glass-walled office filled with professionals from around the world inspired him, reminding him of how far he had come.

In the evenings, he wandered through the city, eager to soak in its wonders.

He visited the British Museum, standing in awe before ancient artefacts that told stories of civilisations long past. He strolled through Hyde Park, golden leaves crunching beneath his feet – a tranquil escape from the bustling city outside.

He marvelled at the lights of Piccadilly Circus, the shops of Oxford Street, and the grandeur of Buckingham Palace. He took a boat ride down the Thames, the city's skyline reflecting in the rippling water.

Every experience filled him with a sense of wonder and humility. He was no longer just a boy from a small village; he was a citizen of the world, expanding his horizons with each step.

A Call Home

One evening, after a long day, Narayan stood on a bridge overlooking the Thames. The water shimmered under the city lights; the wind cooled against his face. He pulled out his phone and dialled home.

His father answered on the first ring. "Narayan! How are you, beta?"

"I'm good, Papa," Narayan said, his voice thick with emotion. "London is… it's everything I imagined and more."

His father's voice softened. "We always knew you would go far. You're living the dream, son."

His mother's voice came through next, warm and comforting. "We miss you, but we know you're where you're meant to be. Your journey is ours, too."

Narayan's heart swelled. "I'll make you proud, Maa."

"You already have," she said, her voice full of love.

As he ended the call, Narayan looked out at the city. The journey had just begun, but he felt a quiet confidence growing within him. He was ready to embrace the future, knowing the love and trust of his family were with him every step of the way.

Wisdom in Unexpected Places

During his time in London, Narayan attended client meetings and networking events. He met people from different walks of life - bankers, entrepreneurs, consultants - all carrying their own stories of success, failure, and resilience.

At a dinner hosted by KrestBnk International, he found himself seated next to **Mr. Neon Anderson**, a retired banker turned mentor. Mr. Anderson's eyes twinkled with experience and humour.

"Enjoying London, young man?" Mr. Anderson asked.

"Yes, sir. It's been an incredible experience."

"Good. But remember, a place is just a backdrop. What matters is the journey you're on and the people you meet."

Narayan nodded, intrigued.

"Don't get so lost in the chase that you forget to live," Mr. Anderson continued. "Success isn't just about titles and salaries. It's about who you become along the way."

Narayan felt a pang in his heart. He thought of his father's words, of Angelina, and of the path he was forging.

"Thank you," he said quietly. "I needed to hear that."

A New Sense of Self

London taught Narayan many things: the importance of adaptability, the richness of diversity, and the thrill of exploration. But more than anything, it gave him a deeper understanding of himself.

He had stepped out of his comfort zone, faced the unknown, and thrived. The boy who once hesitated to dream big was now a man ready to carve his path in the world.

As he prepared to return to India, he felt a profound sense of fulfilment. His family's pride, his own growth, and the experiences he had gathered were treasures he would carry forever.

And with every breath, he knew, this was only the beginning.

A Shift in Perspective

When Narayan returned to Mumbai, he was different. The trip had widened his perspective. He realised that life was more than just achieving goals - it was about growth, connection, and purpose.

He still worked hard, but he began to set boundaries. He took time to read, reflect, and reconnect with old friends. He called his father more often; their conversations filled with warmth and wisdom.

Narayan knew he was still healing, still finding his way. But for the first time in a long while, he felt a sense of balance - a fragile but hopeful equilibrium between ambition and life.

The pain of his past hadn't vanished, but it no longer defined him. He was more than his heartbreak, more than his job title. He was a work in progress, and that was enough.

* * * * *

Chapter 8

The Fall from Greed

Success brought satisfaction, but also a restless craving for more. The thrill of achievement was intoxicating, yet a dangerous whisper began to echo in Narayan's mind: *'What if there's more to be had, faster?'* And with that whisper, a new challenge emerged.

The computer screen's glow cast shadows on Narayan's face as he scrolled through stock charts deep into the night. At ***Apirax Capital***, he had mastered financial analysis and risk management, but now a sharper urge gnawed at him - **greed**.

His achievements felt hollow, eclipsed by a restless craving for *more* - more success, more validation, more proof that he was enough. Late nights bled into dawn, the lines between ambition and desperation blurring.

At first, his personal investments were cautious, driven by research and careful thought. He picked companies with strong fundamentals, and his portfolio grew steadily. But steady growth began to feel too slow. The lure of quick profits dangled in front of him like a shiny prize, just out of reach.

One evening, his colleague **Gajraj** leaned over and whispered, "Have you heard about ***Kranix Ajara Ltd.***? My cousin says it's going to double in a week. Everyone's talking about it."

Narayan hesitated. The stock had been climbing rapidly. He hadn't studied the company thoroughly, but the buzz around it was intoxicating.

"You sure?" Narayan asked, his curiosity piqued.

"Trust me," Gajraj grinned. "It's a *sure shot.*"

The phrase *"sure shot"* echoed in Narayan's mind, a drumbeat of temptation that drowned out the cautious voice of his training. Greed's whisper curled around his thoughts, smooth and insistent.

The Rush of Risk

Narayan leaned back in his office chair, staring at the stock charts on his screen. The lines danced upward, promising quick gains. His usual approach was to research thoroughly, but impatience gnawed at him.

Why wait months for growth when others are making fortunes overnight?

He clicked open a financial forum, reading threads filled with bold claims and success stories. A nagging voice in his mind whispered caution, but he brushed it aside. *Just one risky bet*, he thought. *What's the harm?*.

His father's lessons about patience and discipline flickered briefly in his memory, but he pushed them away. This was his chance to make big money quickly.

With a deep breath, he clicked **"Buy,"** pouring a significant portion of his savings into ***Kranix Ajara Ltd.***

The next morning, the stock soared by 15%. Adrenaline spiked through his veins. Maybe Gajraj was right - maybe he was finally riding the wave he'd been chasing.

Tips flowed like a torrent: whispers, headlines, half-truths. His portfolio ballooned, and so did his confidence. He felt invincible.

Or so he believed.

The Tipping Point

But markets are fickle, and what rises quickly can crash even faster.

On Monday morning, Narayan woke up to a series of urgent news alerts: **"Kranix Ajara Ltd. under investigation for fraud."** The screen blurred as he read the details. The company he had gambled on was collapsing under the weight of its own lies.

He logged into his trading account, his heart pounding. The numbers stared back at him, mocking his confidence. The stock had plummeted by 60% and it was still falling.

His hands trembled as he realised the magnitude of his loss. He had ignored the principles he'd learned, the cautious strategies he had once respected. He had traded his hard-earned knowledge for greed, and now he was paying the price.

The Crash

The losses didn't stop there. The domino effect spread through his portfolio. The other stocks he had bought on flimsy tips were also sinking. In just a few days, he had lost more than half of his savings – a sum that had taken him years to build.

He sat in his small apartment, the silence suffocating him. His computer screen was dark now, as if mourning his failure. He buried his face in his hands, the weight of regret pressing down on him.

How did I let it come to this? The thought clawed at him, each heartbeat a painful reminder of the principles he had ignored.

His mind raced through memories of his father's advice, the cautionary tales about greed, the importance of knowledge, and discipline. He had turned his back on everything he knew to be right.

Tears welled in his eyes. He wasn't just mourning the loss of money; he was mourning the loss of his integrity, his confidence, and his belief in himself.

The hollow quiet of his apartment pressed on Narayan's chest, each breath a struggle against the weight of regret. The charts that once promised fortune were now symbols of recklessness. He closed his eyes, memories of his father's lessons surfacing like fragments of a forgotten map.

"Greed is a storm that destroys everything in its path. Choose wisely, Narayan."

The voice in his mind was gentle but firm. He had strayed far from his roots, but perhaps redemption lay in returning to them.

It was time to stop running and face himself – to rebuild, not for wealth, but for integrity.

Facing the Consequences

That evening, Narayan called his father. His voice shook as he confessed everything - the tips, the greed, the devastating losses.

There was a long pause on the other end. When his father finally spoke, his voice was calm but firm.

"Narayan, wealth built on shortcuts is like a house of cards. It looks impressive, but one wrong move, and it collapses."

"I've failed you, Papa," Narayan whispered, his throat tight.

"No, son," his father said gently. "You've made a mistake. That doesn't make you a failure. What matters is what you learn from it. This loss is painful, but it's also a lesson. Greed will always whisper in your ear. You have to choose whether to listen."

Narayan closed his eyes, his father's words sinking deep. The path ahead was clear, but it wouldn't be easy.

The nights after the financial crash were long and restless, each hour heavy with regret. But as dawn broke one morning, Narayan knew he couldn't stay trapped in that darkness. His father's words echoed in his mind: *"This loss is a lesson. Now, you must choose how to rise from it."*

Rebuilding from the Ashes

The next day, Narayan began the slow process of rebuilding. He sold off the remaining stocks in his portfolio, accepting the losses. He went back to his roots - researching carefully, investing thoughtfully, and ignoring the seductive lure of quick profits.

He started keeping a journal of his trades, writing down his reasons for every decision. Each entry served as a reminder of the importance of discipline, knowledge, and patience.

Over time, his investments grew again - not at the lightning pace he once craved, but steadily and securely. More importantly, *he* grew too. The sting of his losses became a guiding principle: **never trade integrity for greed**.

A Hard-Earned Lesson

One evening, as he looked out at the Mumbai skyline, he reflected on his journey. The pain of his financial crash still lingered, but it no longer defined him. He had faced greed, stumbled, and risen stronger.

In his journal, he wrote:

"Greed may promise riches, but wisdom ensures wealth. True success isn't in quick gains but in lasting growth."

He closed the journal, a sense of calm settling over him. He had lost wealth but found something richer - **wisdom carved from the stone of regret**.

And this time, he knew he wouldn't let it slip away.

With a determined heart, he booked a train back to Sukhpura. He needed to feel the soil beneath his feet, to hear the familiar rustle of the neem tree, and to remind himself of the boy who once dared to dream beyond the fields.

78

* * * * *

Chapter 9

Resolution and Reflection

The sun was setting over the hills of Sukhpura, casting a warm, golden glow over the fields. Narayan stood on the balcony of his childhood home, the familiar scent of earth and blooming jasmine wrapping around him like an old friend. The air was still, the quiet only broken by the distant laughter of children playing in the fields.

He closed his eyes and let the stillness seep into his bones. After years of relentless pursuit - of love, success, and self-worth - he was finally learning to be at peace with the silence.

A Return to Roots

It had been months since his return from London. Narayan's fingers traced the edges of his London boarding pass, the sleekness of the paper a stark contrast to the rough, familiar soil of Sukhpura. The bustling avenues of London, with their endless possibilities, had expanded his world. Yet each step he took in that foreign land seemed to echo with a quiet longing for home.

Growth doesn't mean forgetting where you started, he thought. He needed to stand beneath the neem tree to let the earth of his childhood ground him once more. In that stillness, perhaps he could reconcile ambition with authenticity - a bridge between who he was and who he was becoming.

The weight of the financial crash still clung to him like a shadow, but the distance had reshaped him. Being back in Sukhpura felt like slipping into a well-worn garment - comfortable, familiar, and deeply reassuring. The village, with its timeless rhythm, reminded him of the boy beneath the layers of ambition and heartache.

He walked the dusty paths leading to his old *pathshala*, where his journey had begun. The neem tree still stood tall, its branches swaying gently in the breeze as if whispering secrets only a child could hear. He smiled, the image of his younger self flickering in his mind - hopeful, curious, untouched by the weight of the world.

The memories were no longer jagged fragments of loss. Instead, they were touchstones - markers of resilience and growth. He understood now that healing wasn't about erasing the past. It was about honouring it, allowing those lessons to shape his future.

Conversations with Papa

That evening, as Narayan sat on the porch with his father, a cup of tea warming his hands, the sky was painted with shades of pink and gold. The first stars began to twinkle above, distant yet steady.

His father's gaze rested on him; eyes filled with quiet understanding. "You seem different, Narayan. Calmer."

Narayan nodded, his voice steady. "I've been through so much, Papa. I held onto my pain because I thought it defined me. But I've realised it doesn't. The crash taught me humility, Angelina taught me the courage to love, and each failure taught me the strength to rise again. These moments didn't break me; they shaped me." He paused, his fingers tracing the rim of his cup. "I thought I needed to succeed to prove something - to myself, to the world. But now, I want to succeed because I love the journey, the challenge."

He looked up, his gaze meeting his father's. "You're 54, and I'm half your age. If I can be even half as strong as you one day, Papa, I'll consider that my greatest success."

His father's smile was gentle. "True success comes from within, *beta*. Resilience isn't about never falling; it's about getting back up, learning, and knowing when to let go."

A weight lifted from Narayan's shoulders. He realised he didn't have to carry his past as a burden. It could be a foundation instead - a story of growth, not of loss.

Letting Go

That night, as he lay in his bed, he thought of Angelina. Her memory no longer brought the sharp sting of loss. Instead, it was a gentle ache - a reminder of love, of lessons learned, and of the strength he had discovered within himself.

He whispered a silent wish into the darkness: *I hope you're happy wherever you are.*

He let his mind wander through the corridors of his past - the highs of love, the sting of failure, and the quiet strength of his father's words. Each memory, once a sharp thorn, now felt like a stepping stone. He realised that holding on to pain was like carrying a weight that no longer served him.

With that, he let go of the last thread tethering him to the past. It was time to step forward and embrace the future with open arms.

A New Beginning

Back in Mumbai, Narayan approached his work with renewed clarity. He no longer sought success to prove his worth; he worked for the challenge, the learning, and the growth. His colleagues noticed the shift - a calm confidence that inspired trust and respect.

One day, Clairey, his mentor from London, called with an offer.

"There's a position opening up in our London office," she said.

Narayan listened intently, a quiet sense of purpose anchoring him.

"It's a big step," she continued. "But I believe you're ready."

The old Narayan might have hesitated, tethered by fear of leaving the comfort of familiarity. But as he gazed out at the sunset, casting a warm glow over Sukhpura, he felt the strength of his roots beneath him.

He took a deep breath, the wind carrying the scent of his village – the scent of home.

"I'd love to take it," he replied, his voice steady and resolute.

He thought of the long nights spent doubting himself, of the days when the weight of expectations nearly crushed him. But here, standing on the soil that had taught him resilience, he felt an unshakeable certainty. He wasn't leaving home; he was carrying it with him. Every step he took in London would be guided by the values of **Sukhpura** - patience, resilience, and integrity.

Clairey's voice brightened. "You're going to do great things, Narayan."

As he hung up the phone, he let the moment settle around him. The horizon stretched out before him, vast and promising. This time, he wasn't running away from his past. He was stepping forward, guided by the wisdom and resilience he had gained.

That evening, as Narayan walked back to his apartment, each step was a quiet promise - to his family, his dreams, and to himself. The winds of resilience, which had once carried him through the fiercest storms, now propelled him towards boundless horizons.

Reflections on the Journey

As Narayan stood beneath the ancient neem tree in Sukhpura, the memories of his journey swirled in his mind like autumn leaves caught in a breeze. The rough bark under his fingertips anchored him, reminding him of where he began. The weight of past failures and losses pressed against his chest, but here, surrounded by the familiar stillness of home, those burdens felt lighter.

He closed his eyes, breathing in the scents of earth, jasmine, and distant smoke. The whispers of his childhood echoed in the rustling leaves - the laughter of his friends, the firm voice of his father, the warmth of simpler times.

A quiet thought surfaced: *"I am not my failures. I am not defined by what I've lost. I am the boy who climbed trees, who dreamed beyond these fields, who dared to love and stumble. And I am still standing."*

He knelt and pressed a small stone into the soil beneath the neem tree - the same stone he'd carried since his first day of school. It was a piece of his younger self - a symbol of unwavering determination, of a boy who dared to dream beyond his circumstances. By returning it to the earth, he honoured the past while making room for the future.

"Let this stay here," he whispered. "A reminder that no matter how far I go, I am always part of this soil."

As he rose, a gentle breeze swept through the branches, rustling the leaves in quiet agreement. The wind carried away the fragments of doubt and fear. He turned towards the horizon.

With roots deep, spirit unbroken, and eyes fixed ahead, Narayan was ready. The winds of resilience would carry him forward – through every new beginning.

* * * * *